This is one of a series of books specially prepared for very young children.

The simple text tells the story of each picture and the bright, colourful illustrations will promote lively discussion between child and adult.

British Library Cataloguing in Publication Data

Haselden, Mary
 Look at me. — (Ladybird toddler books)
 1. Readers — 1950-
 I. Title II. Breeze, Lynn
 428.6 PE1119
 ISBN 0-7214-0853-2

First edition

Published by Ladybird Books Ltd Loughborough Leicestershire UK
Ladybird Books Inc Lewiston Maine 04240 USA

Printed in England

Ladybird Toddler Books

look at me

written by MARY HASELDEN
illustrated by LYNN BREEZE

Ladybird Books

Look at me!
I have a head and a body,
two arms and
two legs.

So do I.

I have two eyes, two ears,
a nose and a mouth.

So do I.

Look at me!
I have fair hair
and green
eyes.

I can stand on my head.

Watch me!
I can get dressed
by myself.

I can fasten my shoes.

Look at me!
I'm helping to wash
the dishes.

I'm cleaning the floor.

Look at me!
I can run faster than anyone.

Watch me!
I can climb up very high.

I can catch a ball.

I can kick a ball.
Watch!

I'm pushing my sister.

I'm pushing my brother.
Watch!

Look at me helping
with the shopping.

This is a very heavy bag.

Watch me eating my lunch.
I can eat it all up.

I'm drinking my milk.

Look at me!
I'm painting a picture.

Look at mine!

Look at me!
I'm driving a racing car.

I'm a doctor.

Watch me feed the ducks.

Look at me swinging very high.

Look at me!
I can cook...

...and I like to lick the spoon.

Watch me help
to bath the baby.
Splash! Splash!

I've coloured a picture…

...and I'm writing my name.
Look!

I went to playgroup today.
Look what I made!

Look at me!
I'm ready for bed.
Now I can have a story.